Coco
My Delicious Life

READ ALL THE LOTUS LANE BOOKS!

LOTUS LANE

Coco

My
Delicious
Life

by Kyla May

BRANCHES

SCHOLASTIC INC.

To my gorgeous girls, Jaida, Kiara, and Mikka,
who give me such inspiration and love.
I'm so lucky to have you three.
Love, Mummy xxx

No part of this publication may be reproduced, stored in a retrieval system, or transmitted in any form or by any means, electronic, mechanical, photocopying, recording, or otherwise, without written permission of the publisher. For information regarding permission, write to Scholastic Inc., Attention: Permissions Department, 557 Broadway, New York, NY 10012.

Library of Congress Cataloging-in-Publication Data
May, Kyla. Coco: my delicious life / by Kyla May.
p. cm. — (Lotus Lane ; 2)
Summary: Coco, one of the Lotus Lane Girls, loves cooking and animals, so when the club decides to plant a vegetable garden to help save snails, organizing a cupcake sale is an obvious idea—but Mika, the new girl next door, is still an unresolved problem.
Includes cupcake recipe.
ISBN 978-0-545-44514-6 (pbk.) — ISBN 978-0-545-49615-5 (hardback) —ISBN 978-0-545-49681-0 (ebook)
1. Baking—Juvenile fiction. 2. Gardening—Juvenile fiction. 3. Best friends—Juvenile fiction.
4. Friendship—Juvenile fiction. 5. Neighbors—Juvenile fiction. 6. Elementary schools—Juvenile fiction.
7. Diary fiction. [1. Baking—Fiction. 2. Gardening—Fiction. 3. Best friends—Fiction. 4. Friendship—Fiction.
5. Neighbors—Fiction. 6. Elementary schools—Fiction. 7. Schools—Fiction. 8. Diaries—Fiction.] I. Title.
PZ7.M4535Coc 2013
813.6--dc23
2012035576

ISBN 978-0-545-49615-5 (hardcover) / ISBN 978-0-545-44514-6 (paperback)

12 11 10 9 8 7 6 5 4 3 2 1   13 14 15 16 17 18/0

Printed in China
First Scholastic printing, July 2013

38

TABLE OF CONTENTS

THIS
DIARY
BELONGS TO
Coco

Chapter 1

Yay!

WOOT WOOT CLAP

Thursday

This diary is dedicated to Evie (Full name: Evie Evionelli Cannoli Canino), my Chihuahua, without whom none of this would be possible. At all. Not even a little bit.

Not even sure why we're talking about it — that's how impossible it would be.

Big round of applause for Evie . . .
Woot! Woot!

1

Dear Diary,

Welcome to your first day of work (as my diary). Since I already know everything about you (you're yellow and purple, you have 96 pages, a picture of me is taped on your cover, and most of all, you enjoy reading), why don't I tell you a little bit about MYSELF?

My parents got you for me because my BFF, Kiki, got a diary from her mom. Both Lulu (our other BFF) and I thought it was ultra cool. So when my painting of Evie won an award at the school art fair for "most lifelike" they knew exactly what to get for me as a reward: <u>You!</u>

My painting looks pretty lifelike, right?

MOST LIFELIKE

EVIE ROCKS!
BEST DOG EVER!

Poor Lulu . . . I hope her parents catch on soon. She really wants a diary, too!

Here are some things you might want to know about me...

AMO:

AMO= Italian for "I love"

✓ Animals

✓ Gardening
✓ Digging in the dirt

✓ Baking

My cupcakes are so yummy, if I do say so myself.

✓ Lotus Lane Girls Club

LOTUS LANE

✓ Climbing trees

NOT SO MUCH:

✗ Multiplication tables
✗ Fashion

Fashion is super-duper-luper important to my BFFs – Kiki (the one with the diary) and Lulu.

This is Kiki. She is a fashion star. ➡️

KIKI

And here is Lulu. She is quite a planner and a movie star know-it-all.

LULU

All three of us have dogs. Kiki's dog is named Maxi, and Lulu's dog is named Bosco. (Bosco is really a cat who thinks she's a dog.)

Maxi

Evie

Bosco

We all live close to one another on Lotus Lane. Lotus Lane is the prettiest street in Amber Acres!

KIKI'S HOUSE

MY HOUSE

LULU'S HOUSE

The three of us invented the LLGC (which stands for Lotus Lane Girls Club!) because we wanted to make time to do lots of really cool things together. And now we do!

THIS IS A LOTUS FLOWER

LOTUS LANE

Check out our weekly calendar of activities on the next page. As you can see, we're very busy. My super-duper-est activity is Cupcake Catch-Up. Since baking is my favorite thing to do, I get to be in charge of that activity.

LOTUS LANE

	MONDAY	TUESDAY	WEDNESDAY
Club Name	Super Scrapbooking	Doggie Day Spa	Ten-Minute Makeover
Club Activity	Create scrapbooks pages	Pamper our pets	Do manicure: pedicures, and style our hair
Club Location	KiKi's house	Coco's backyard	Lulu's bedroom

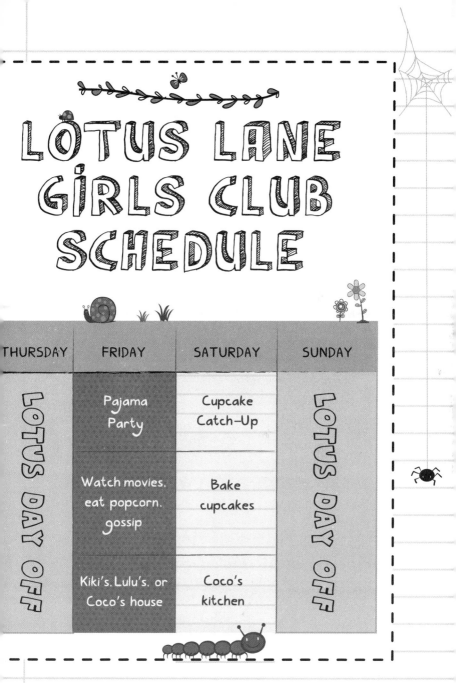

LOTUS LANE GIRLS CLUB SCHEDULE

THURSDAY	FRIDAY	SATURDAY	SUNDAY
LOTUS DAY OFF	Pajama Party	Cupcake Catch-Up	LOTUS DAY OFF
	Watch movies, eat popcorn, gossip	Bake cupcakes	
	Kiki's, Lulu's, or Coco's house	Coco's kitchen	

So back to me . . .

I'm an only child, but I'm never alone because I have a GIANT Italian family — the biggest one I know. I have two nonnas and nonnos (grandmas and grandpas), 20 uncles and aunties, and 40 cousins. Even though they all have their own houses, they're always in my kitchen cooking. With all that coming and going, we go through six doormats a year!

So there you have it, Diary. Coco in a nutshell. I can't wait to show you to Kiki and Lulu tomorrow! Night!

Chapter 2

Sequins, Snails, and Sleeping Bags

Friday

Diary, did you hear my dad come into
our room and kiss me good-bye before?
It was so early, I think I thought I
was still dreaming.

I wish I had been more awake. You
see, he's a scientist and he goes
on trips to save insects and animals
around the world. This time he's
off to save the snail!

What's that you say, Diary? Oh, I completely agree – it is _so_ sad that the snail is becoming **extinct**! If I had been more awake, I would have asked Dad to tell me more about this trip . . . and about those snails!

EXTINCT = when a whole species of animal or insect is completely wiped out forever

SAVE THE SNAIL

HELP ME!

Off to school. So excited it's Friday! Tonight, it's my turn to host the LLGC Pajama Party! I'm going to make the theme Happy Planet so I can tell Kiki and Lulu all about those poor snails!

LLGC PAJAMA PARTY

Hi again, Diary!

Kiki and Lulu are fast asleep here in my bedroom. But I'm too excited to even just close my eyes. I think it's because we came up with an idea on how to help the snails!

Well, let me back up for a second. FIRST, I had to get them to listen to me talk about the snails, which wasn't as easy as it sounds. . . .

"We need to think of a way to help save the snail." — me

"Can you make the TV louder?" — Lulu

"You can make it as loud as you want, it's not going to make Elke Eden's gown any prettier." — Kiki

"You are SO right about that. . . . This red carpet stinks." — Lulu

"Click" — the TV, as I shut it off

That sure got their attention! Then I told them that snails live in vegetable gardens.

"We should plant a vegetable garden and fill it with the snails my dad brings back." — me

"We could grow tomatoes!" — Lulu

"And carrots!" — me

"If only we could grow sequins!" — Kiki

Kiki can have a one-track mind. It's okay though. Fashion is her passion, just like animals are mine.

Once we had a plan going, we watched the rest of the live red-carpet show.

Then Kiki and Lulu fell asleep. But my head was spinning with vegetables! And I just couldn't wait to tell you the . . .

Oooh . . . dozed off there for a second . . .

. . . the news . . . Couldn't wait to tell you the <u>news</u> about deciding to plant a vegetable garden!!!

I guess now that I have told you, I can fall asleep. Night night, Diary.

Chapter 3

Cupcakes Make the World Go 'Round

Saturday

AWESOMENESS! Guess what?
You'll never guess!

Fine, I'll give you a teeny-tiny hint. It has to do with running into Principal Morton. Mom and I ran into him while we were shopping at the local farmers market. He asked me what was new, and I told him about how the LLGC is trying to plant a garden to help save the snails. You won't believe this, but he said we should plant our vegetable garden at school! How cool is that?!

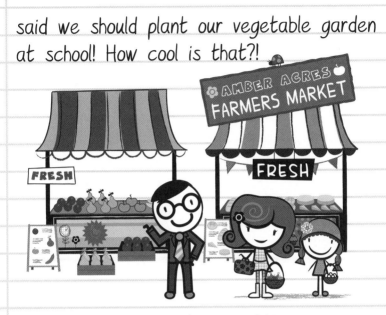

He says we'd have to raise the money ourselves, but . . . details, details . . . The point is we can plant the garden. Now the snails will have a place to live. Yippee! I can't wait to tell Kiki and Lulu!!

Okay, but, how <u>are</u> we going to raise the money?

i know what to do!

I'm sure Lulu will know just what to do! She loves to problem-solve and plan things! And she'll add a touch of glamour, too.

Okay, time for Cupcake Catch-Up . . . Today we're going to make the simple but classic World-Famous Coco Cupcake, otherwise known as vanilla vanilla (what can I say, I ♥ vanilla)! Check out my recipe on the next page.

I ♥ VANILLA VANILLA CUPCAKES

Ingredients

Cake:

1 cup white sugar
1/2 cup butter
2 eggs
1-1/2 cups all-purpose flour

1-3/4 teaspoons baking powder
1/2 cup milk

Frosting:

2 cups powdered sugar
2 tablespoons butter

2 tablespoons milk
1/2 teaspoon vanilla

Directions

Cake:

Preheat oven to 350 degrees F.*
Line a muffin pan with liners.

In a medium bowl, mix the sugar and butter. Beat in the eggs, one at a time.

Combine flour and baking powder, then add to sugar and butter mixture, and mix well.

Stir in milk until butter mixture is smooth. Spoon batter into liners.

Bake 20 to 25 minutes.* Let cool.

*Ask an adult for help when using the oven.

Frosting:

Combine ingredients and beat until fluffy. Frost!

Lulu had an awesome idea for a **fund-raiser**. See? I knew she would know what to do!

FUND-RAISER = an event to raise money (or funds) for something

"Why not run a cupcake stand on Lotus Lane? You ARE the cupcake queen after all!" – Lulu

(She's right about that!)

Lulu figured out how much money we could make at a cupcake stand:

Bake 25 cupcakes each
That's 75 altogether
Charge $3 a piece
$3 x 75 = $225!
$225 = enough to buy supplies for a new vegetable garden!

And Kiki said we could use her parents' card table for the stand. LLGC decided we would all work together on our Save the Snails cupcake stand. Kiki and Lulu are the BEST!!! **BTW**: We always support one another's causes. That's what BFFs do!

SAVE
THE
SNAIL

BTW =
by the way

Chapter 4

Here Kitty, Kitty . . .

Sunday

I was just about to look up info on
the snail when I remembered that Mom
is having a family dinner tonight. She
wanted EVERYONE in the family to see
my painting of Evie.

Maybe this would
be a good time
to introduce
you to my
family?

Dad   Me   Mom

Evie

MY BIG FAMILY:

Nonno Nico

Nonna Nicci

Uncle Nick

Aunt Nicolina

Cousin Nick

Cousin Nicoletta

Cousin Nicola

If you're ever wondering where to find my family members, just follow the delicious smells coming from my kitchen.

Hmm . . . I think it's time for _me_ to follow those delicious smells. . . .

MY HOUSE

yum

delicious

Dinner was really fun! Mom put Evie's portrait on an easel and covered it with a sheet. Before dessert, she said, "Please turn your attention to this magnificent painting painted by our very own Coco." Then she whisked the sheet off the easel. "Ta-da!" she said. Everybody clapped and cheered which made me feel special and loved. (And kind of like a famous painter – for a second anyway.)

Before

After

After dinner, I went out to sit in my favorite spot in our backyard. My new next-door neighbor Mika came over to pick up her dog's chew toy (it must've come over the fence). I can't believe she had the nerve to step foot in MY yard!

Mika moved to a house on Lotus Lane (in between me and Kiki) only two weeks ago. Since then, she's already said something nasty to Kiki about her art project. She also borrowed Kiki's dog, Maxi, for the school fashion parade without asking.

(Mika said she thought Kiki gave her permission, and Kiki ended up believing Mika. But as Kiki's fellow LLGC girls, Lulu and I have our doubts.)

Also, as Lulu pointed out recently, Mika's been hanging around Mega Meanie, Queen of Mean, Katy Krupski. If that's not proof of her meanness, then I don't know what is!

As I was sitting in my fave spot, you'll never guess who wandered up to me, but the cutest, cuddliest kitten in the whole wide world!! This is what she looked like.

You'll notice that she has no collar. Know what that means? She probably has no owner. This is what she would look like if she *were* owned by someone:

Doesn't she look happier?

And look how happy Evie would look with a new sister!

And now look how happy everyone is in this picture:

A girl can dream, can't she?! ☺

You want to hear something weird, though? When Nonna saw me playing with the kitty, she quickly pulled me inside the house and told me to stay away from black cats.

This is what Nonna looks like worried:

This is what Nonna looks like the rest of the time:

As my mother would say:

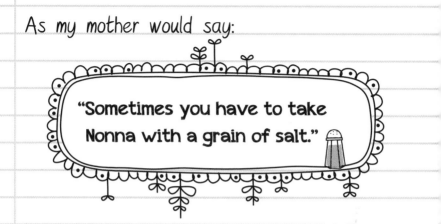

"Sometimes you have to take
Nonna with a grain of salt."

That means I shouldn't take Nonna too seriously. Which is good, because I wouldn't want to stay away from that kitten . . . she was WAAAAAAY too cute!

Now back to my computer and looking up the snail's favorite foods! See you tomorrow, Diary!

Hot dogs?

Sprinkles?

Mushrooms?

Chili?

Chocolate

Chapter 5

Eenie Meanie Mika Mo

Monday

Horror of horrors, Diary!

Miss Humphries paired us up today for a history project and you'll never guess who my partner is! Actually, it's someone you've never met before, so you really will never guess unless I tell you. Mika Maeda. That's who!

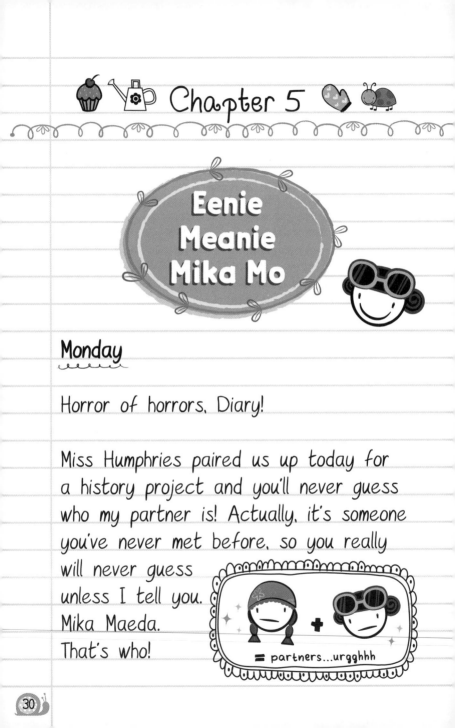

= partners...urgghhh

Miss Humphries wants us to interview our partners about their family **traditions**. We have to write a report about them by next Monday. That means a whole week of working with Mika. . . .

TRADITION =
a custom or routine passed down within a family, society, or culture

And as if all of this isn't bad enough — while I'm stuck all by myself with Eenie Meanie Mika Mo, Kiki and Lulu get to be partners! They are going to have the best time EVER . . . without me. It's not fair. ☹

At least I get to see them tonight at Super Scrapbooking at Kiki's house. Gotta run!

Well, Super Scrapbooking was awesome (as usual). I feel so much better now that I've spent some time with my LLGC girls.
Kiki made today's theme Save the Snail! And we had all kinds of cool snail stickers and vegetable stickers and flower stickers! Check out my scrapbook pages:

Wow! Scrapbooking tires me out! So does worrying about meanies like Mika – I hope she won't be too mean to me, Diary.

Chapter 6

My Flavorite

Tuesday

I just came from Doggie Day Spa, which was spa-tacular! Kiki made some great outfits for the dogs (and for Bosco!). And Lulu worked her magic with the BeDazzler. It's amazing what a few beads on the collar can do!

Check out these photos from today:

If only that black kitten had come back for Doggie Day Spa — she'd look so pretty in a sparkly new collar!

But more important, we chose flavors for the cupcakes we're going to sell at our Save the Snails stand. Here is the **exclusive** worldwide premiere of the first LLGC Cupcake Stand's cupcake flavor lineup. . . .

EXCLUSIVE =
shutting out all others; special

Red Velvet with Cream Cheese Frosting
by Lulu

Chocolate with Chocolate Frosting
by Kiki

Carrot with Cream Cheese Frosting
by Chef Coco
(You can never have too much cream cheese frosting!)

These cupcakes will all be topped with chocolate (soil-colored!) sprinkles!

Wow! Just thinking about all these plans is making me dizzy. We have a lot to do in a short bit of time. . . . The cupcake stand is on Sunday. And Sunday is only _five_ days away!

Guess it's time for beddy-bye.

Chapter 7

The Good, the Bad, and the Katy

Wednesday

Today during lunch Miss Melody let us stay in the classroom and use art supplies to make posters for the cupcake stand.
BTW, Miss Melody is our art teacher and she's the BEST!!

MISS MELODY

Look how great our posters turned out!

Then this happened:

"Coco, did you know Kiki's grandmother's grandmother was a lady-in-waiting for Queen Elizabeth? That's why Kiki's mother became a fashion stylist — to keep up the family tradition!" — **Lulu**

"Or that Lulu does this amazing thing that she never bothered telling you about?!" — **Kiki**

"Or that we're having more fun than you because we're working with each other and getting even closer and you have to work with Mika?!" — **Kiki and Lulu**

That was the not-so-good part of our poster-making lunch. (Okay, maybe they didn't say ALL those things, but you get the idea.)

And, well, they did actually tell me that they really missed having me around. So that made me feel a little bit better. Like this little. But not as better as I'd feel if suddenly Miss Melody said we could all three work together.

THEN Katy Krupski came into the room to ask Miss Melody something. Katy must have overheard us talking about the cupcake stand because then this happened:

"Oh, Coco, I hope you'll be buying the cupcakes and not actually making them yourself. I've tasted yours and, well..." – Katy

Then Katy even scrunched up her nose!!

Then Miss Melody said something my mother says a lot: "Now, Katy . . ."

"If you don't have anything nice to say, then don't say anything at all."

I was glad Miss Melody said that to Katy. But then I started to wonder if maybe my cupcakes ARE stinky. But Lulu and Kiki promised me that they're not.

After school, we had our Ten-Minute Makeover club at Lulu's. We all agreed that it's not a very good sign that Mika is friends with Katy. But I still have to work with Mika on the history project, so . . . well, so, nothing, I guess.

Lulu gave us shimmery manicures in colors that match our cupcakes! And she glued a matching bead to each of our pinkie fingernails!

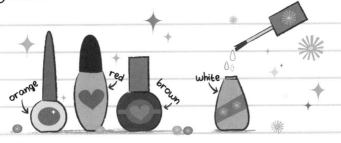

At dinner, I asked Nonna why she was so worried about the black cat the other night. Nonna said that her mother had taught her that black cats were bad luck. (You could say this belief was a tradition in her family!) Please don't tell Nonna, but I think her tradition is a little silly.

Look at me thinking about traditions — SCHOOLWORK — in my free time! Ugh.

Speaking of schoolwork, I have to go to Mika's house after school tomorrow to work on the history project. NOT looking forward to that!! Okay, Diary . . . sleep tight.

But, Diary, what if it's not a silly tradition? What if it's true? Now it's me who's being silly.

Okay, but there is a lot of proof pointing to the fact that since I saw that black cat, I've had some bad luck:

1. I got paired with Mika.
2. Katy Krupski was mean to me.
3. I can't think of anything else yet, but that doesn't mean it isn't about to happen!

Chapter 8

Maybe I Lika Mika

Thursday

DIARY! ARE YOU OKAY? Nothing bad has happened to you since the last time we chatted, right? No one tried to read you, right? Okay, good! Oh, Diary . . . I've gone from thinking Nonna's belief is silly to thinking I'm crazy for <u>not</u> believing it. As long as the cupcake stand goes okay on Sunday and my history project goes okay on Monday, then everything will be fine.

Well, and also as long as my dad is able to rescue the snails. And as long as Kiki and Lulu still want to spend time with me even though I'm not doing the history project with them. Geez . . . that's a lot of "as long as" things. . . .

Okay, I guess I should go to school now. . . .

Kiki and Lulu didn't think I should worry about the black cat. That made me feel a little better.

But then I reminded them about my having to work with Mika and about what Katy Krupski said. They saw my point about the bad luck. Now they think I should be afraid. Very afraid! And guess what? I totally am!

EEK

It's time to go to Mika's house. I would do ANYTHING not to go, but I have to. Kiki and Lulu are meeting up at Lulu's house now. Why couldn't I be going there instead?!! Hopefully they won't do anything too fun without me. I'll let you know what happens.

What happened was that I had fun! At least I think I did. . . When I got there, Mika asked me to take off my shoes.

Her house was quiet. It's the opposite of my house, which is always SO loud.

She took me to her bedroom and the moment I saw the Sleuth Sally poster on her bedroom wall, I knew that I was probably going to start liking her.

The LLGC has seen every SS movie like a hundred times!

Also, Mika has a Kokeshi doll collection, which is really cool. When my dad went to Japan to save a moth, he brought back a Kokeshi doll for me, too! So I guess we have some things in common. And I liked doing the project with her, because I learned a lot of new things about Japanese traditions. For example . . .

my Kokeshi doll

1. Whenever she sees her grandparents from Japan, she bows to them before she says anything. Her relatives from Japan all bow to one another. (If my whole family bowed to one another, we'd run out of time to talk to one another!)

2. In Japan, you're not supposed ACHOO!! to sneeze in public. (Whenever I hold in a sneeze, I'm afraid my ears will explode!)

3. Some Japanese people keep special slippers in the bathroom — so that no one wears the same shoes in the bathroom that they wear anywhere else. (If you ask me, that's a really smart idea!)

We were having a good time. So I told her about the cupcake stand, and also about what my nonna said about the black cat.

And you know what, Diary? Mika gave me something. It's a small plastic black cat called a Maneki Neko cat.  It's supposed to keep bad luck away. She's letting me borrow it until after the cupcake stand. (It looks like the lost kitten!)

Mika even offered to help us with the stand – Katy would never be so kind. I almost said OfCoursePleaseWe NeedAllTheHelpWeCanGet, but then I realized that Lulu might not like that. So I said:

"Thank you so much for offering, but there isn't really much left to do."

Which made me feel:

SAD

Chapter 9

Lulu, We Made a Boo-Boo

Friday

Coco: No new bad luck so far. U?

Lulu: Me neither.

Kiki: I had bad luck. dad dropped eggs while making brkfst.

Kiki: JK!!! so sick of eggs. was totes good luck! haha!

JK = just kidding

49

At lunch, the LLGC sat together and we talked about plans for tonight's sleepover at Lulu's house. We're going to watch **Sleuth Sally & the Missing Cocoon**, where Sally shrinks down to the size of a ladybug. Mika passed by our table and waved. Kiki and I waved back. But Lulu shot us a death look!! So

we put our hands down right away. But I don't really think Lulu's anti-Mikaness is fair — it's all because of Mika's friendship with Katy.

Like my mother always says:

"You can't judge a book by its cover."

What's that, Diary? You think I should say something to Lulu? I agree. It is the right thing to do. But what if I'm too scared?

Right again, Diary. There's no reason to be scared. After all, Lulu is one of my BESTEST friends in the whole wide world and a LLGC member on top of that!!

Before our sleepover, Kiki and Lulu and I went around the neighborhood, hanging up our posters for the cupcake stand. I almost talked to Lulu then, but I chickened out at the last second.

I still kept cheering myself on though, and by the time we had finished watching **Sleuth Sally**, I finally got up the courage to tell Lulu that I think she should give Mika a chance.

I told her and Kiki that I think we made a mistake about Mika, that she seems really friendly, and that she even offered to help us with the cupcake stand.

> "That was sweet of mika!"
> – Kiki

> "   " – Lulu

I guess Lulu didn't know what to say. Then Lulu and Kiki went to sleep because we have a big, super-long day of Cupcake Catch-Up tomorrow. I'll keep working on Lulu. Time to get some sleep myself . . . I can't believe that when I wake up tomorrow, it'll already be baking day!

NIGHTY NIGHT

Chapter 10

Not on the List

Saturday

Lulu sent me a list of things we need for Cupcake Catch-Up today.

Oh no . . . Now Lulu just sent a list of all of our lists!

Lulu: Coco here's the list of baking items. ♡ ♡

flour, sugar, eggs, milk, chocolate, carrots, cream cheese, baking powder, butter, muffin-pan liners

Okay . . . she just sent me a text reminding me to check my lists. Can you say cuckoo bananas!?

I better go gather up the ingredients before Lulu and Kiki get here.

Bad luck update:
1. doggie drama
2. floor full o' fudge batter
3. carrots carrots oh my
4. much much more

Here's what happened earlier:

Kiki and Lulu arrived. I went out back to pick carrots from the vegetable garden while they set up the kitchen. Evie came outside with me. Then the black cat reappeared! Evie saw her and then she went, you guessed it . . . CUCKOO BANANAS!!!!!!

Evie started chasing the cat through the garden, messing up the entire veggie patch and stomping on the carrots! The carrots got bruised all over.

As if that wasn't <u>enough</u> bad luck, then Maxi heard Evie (<u>from two</u> houses over!). He came running into my vegetable garden . . . digging up the dirt and bruising the carrots even more. I couldn't get the animals to calm down.

Finally, Kiki heard me yelling and went to the window. When she saw what Maxi was doing, she raced outside, sideswiping the chocolate batter mixing bowl, making it fly up into the air, turn over, and land – batter side – on Lulu's head!!

Then, that thud made Lulu accidentally pour the whole container of salt into the cream cheese frosting (like a hundred tablespoons worth)!! We had to throw the whole thing out.

Next, my mom came running into the yard with Lulu behind her. I opened my mouth to explain, but before I could even get out a word, I made a funny hiccup sound that turned into a **sob**.

SOB = to cry really hard

That sob turned into another sob and another and before long Kiki and Lulu were sobbing, too, and suddenly the three of us were drowning in a puddle of our own tears.

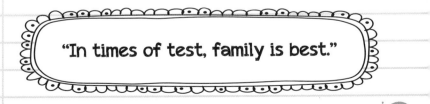

"What are we going to do?" — **Kiki**

"It's already getting dark out!" — **Lulu**

"We'll never get the cupcakes baked in time! Nonna was right — that cat is bad luck!" — **me**

Then my mother said something really smart:

"In times of test, family is best."

As leader of the LLGC Cupcake Stand, I felt it was time to take action. I stood up on my picnic table.

> My mom's right. We're family. Now is the time for us to show what we're made of, for us to band together like a family, and by gosh, for us to fight this bad luck one cupcake at a time. Do it for each other, Lotus Lane Girls Club ... do it for the garden snails!

I stepped off the picnic table. Then I quickly stepped back up.

> If anyone sees that cat coming near this garden between now and the end of the sale ... SEND HER AWAY AS FAST AS YOU CAN! I DON'T CARE HOW CUTE SHE IS! SNAILS ARE AT STAKE!

There was clapping and woot-wooting.
Then I started laughing, and Kiki and Lulu
started laughing. There was so much noise
coming from my backyard that Mika looked
out her bedroom window to see
what was going on. I waved for
her to come over.

The good news:
Because of everything, Lulu
has given Mika permission to help with the
cupcake stand.

It took us a long time to bring Mika up to
speed, because we kept on laughing. But
finally we got the whole story out. And
you know what, Diary?

Mika had everything we were missing!
Carrots, cream cheese, and salt! She
brought it all over along with enough
green tea to make twenty-five
green tea cupcakes of her own.

We were all tired and giggly when we finished icing the last cupcake. But do you know how many cupcakes we have for the cupcake stand tomorrow, Diary?

100! 100 perfect, gorgeous, scrumdiddlyumptious cupcakes! Phew . . . Well, at least Evie and Maxi scared off the black cat. Let's just cross our fingers (and our toes, arms, eyes, and anything else that can be crossed) that our bad luck is over.

For good.

Or at least until after we've sold every cupcake. Oh, and until after the history project is finished. And after everything else important that could happen. Which I guess is just another way of saying for good!

Chapter 11

Sweet Smell of Success

Sunday

The cupcake stand was a huge hit!
We sold every cupcake! We made $300!!!!

$300!!!

My relatives bought lots of cupcakes. And Mika stopped by to help out for a while.

And there were no black cats anywhere!

Now Dad's snails will have a veggie garden to call their very own!!! Long live the snails!!!

Well, homework calls. . . . My history project is due <u>tomorrow</u>, so I better hit the books!

You know who I really like, Diary? Mika.

And you know why I really like her, Diary? Because she's a <u>good</u> person. Katy Krupski or no Katy Krupski, Mika is very sweet. Sometimes, she even saves the day. . . . Oh, and her family traditions are pretty cool, too.

On my way up to my room to do homework, I saw out the window that our S.O.S. (Save Our Snails) sign was caught in one of our trees. When I went outside to get it, I heard meowing — the black kitten!!!

The kitty seemed so scared and lost! And I felt soooo badly about what I said about her yesterday. Then I worried that somehow she knew what I said — she did wait until the sale was over to come back! (But that's cuckoo bananas, right?)

So I rescued the cat (and the sign). But then I was walking to go in the back door when I realized I had never taken the money from the stand inside with me.

After all that work we did, how could I have been so silly?! I looked all over the yard for the money bag but there was no sign of it anywhere!

Coco_Lulu_Kiki_msg

Coco: Any1 take the $ bag home with them?

Kiki: Not Me

Lulu: U LOST the $ bag?!?!

Coco: Not helpful, L.

Lulu: Maybe Mika took it? Just like she took Maxi the day of the fashion parade?!

Just then, as if she could hear what we were texting, Mika came into my yard. And she was carrying the money bag!!!!! I tried not to get angry, but it was hard.

"Mika, what are you—" – me

"Coco, wait, I can explain — I saw the money bag left out on the cupcake stand. I took it for safekeeping." — Mika

Those were the best twenty-one words I heard all day. (Well, except for when Lulu had said the words "Three. Hundred. Dollars!")

When I asked Mika why she hadn't just brought it inside earlier, she said she was **intimidated** by ALL of my relatives. I guess they were being noisy, and Mika is shy.

INTIMIDATED = scared or frightened

Thank goodness the money was safe! Mika to the rescue — again!

The black kitten semed really lonely so Mika and I made a little bed for her in my bedroom.

Then I told Mika that I had to go finish my report. She said she did, too. "Do you think we'll get a good grade?" I asked her.

"I hope so," she said. "I did learn a lot of cool things about your family."

"Me, too – about yours," I told her.

I think we'll get good grades, but like my mother always says,

"You should never count your chickens before they hatch."

Finally, I've finished my report. I am soooooo ready for sleep. So is the kitty.

If only I could keep her! But I don't think Nonna would like that. I just wish there was some way to show Nonna that the kitty doesn't bring bad luck with her.

Sleep tight! Don't let the garden snails bite!

Chapter 12

Sharing Is Caring

Monday

Best Day Ever!

For our history project, Miss Humphries asked each student to tell the class the most interesting tradition we learned about our partner.

"Mika bows to her grandparents before she speaks to them." — me

"Coco's family eats fruits and vegetables from their garden." – **Mika**

"Lulu's family starts every day with a to-do list." – **Kiki**

Mom	Dad	Lulu
☑	☑	☑
☑	☑	☑
☑	☑	☑
☑	☑	☑
☑	☑	

"Every time a baby girl is born in Kiki's family, the new baby is given a pearl necklace from her grandmother that gets added on to on each birthday." – **Lulu**

Grades will be handed out tomorrow. I hope Miss Humphries likes my report!!

At lunch, I invited Mika to sit with us. Just then, Katy Krupski walked over and asked Mika to sit with her! "I'm sorry, Katy, but I'm sitting with Coco, Kiki, and Lulu today," Mika said. I don't know if I would have had the courage to say that to Katy. But I'm really glad Mika did—and in a friendly way, too.

Mika brought sushi for lunch today, and she let us each try a piece. <u>DEEELISH!</u>

Kiki made a drawing of sushi in her sketchbook. She said she was going to start brainstorming sushi-inspired fashion designs! Oh, Kiki!!

Once we were done eating, the four of us went to the library together to learn more about snails' favorite veggies. . . .

1. cucumbers
2. lettuce
3. carrots
4. spinach

I'll have to be sure to buy those types of veggie plants tonight. Uncle Nick is taking me to the **nursery** to pick up the seedlings for our school garden. I'm so excited!!!! I can't wait to plant them at school <u>tomorrow</u>! Yay!

NURSERY = place where young plants are grown

But first, Super Scrapbooking at Kiki's. Gotta run!

Super Scrapbooking was the best! We printed out photos from the cupcake stand. Check out my pages:

And something REALLY big happened, too. Check this out:

"It's a good thing Mika gave me that plastic good luck cat — who knows if the cupcake stand would have been such a success without it?" — me

"I don't even want to think about it." — Kiki

"You guys . . . you know, it wasn't Mika's plastic cat that brought good luck." — Lulu

"Here we go again . . ." — me

(Okay, I didn't actually say that. . . . But I thought it!)

"I'm not saying it was the plastic cat that brought bad luck, exactly. Even though that whole doggie drama happened after Coco borrowed the cat. But really, if anything, it was Mika who brought us good luck." — Lulu

I could hardly believe my ears! But Lulu was right. The doggie disaster, which almost ruined the cupcake stand, did happen after Mika gave me the plastic cat. But when Mika showed up we got back on track for the sale. Then she helped us make more money than we ever would have made without her. And she kept the money safe for us so it wouldn't get stolen.

> "Does this mean Mika can help us plant the vegetable garden tomorrow, Lulu?" — me

Lulu thought for a minute. Kiki and I swapped question-mark looks.

> "Oh...all right..." — Lulu

Did you hear that, Diary? She said, "Oh all right!" That means, OH. ALL. RIGHT. In other words . . .

Yes!!!!

I'm so happy Lulu has at least agreed to give Mika a chance! Who knows . . . maybe one day Lulu will think of Mika as a friend. That's a <u>BIG</u> maybe, but still, that would be a great day!

Okay, now I'm off to the nursery with Uncle Nick and then Mom said I have to go straight to bed. I'm going to need all my energy tomorrow to plant our veggie garden! AND THEN I'm going to need even more energy later for jumping up and down, cartwheeling, and doing my happy dance when Dad walks through the door! I cannot wait to tell him all about the vegetable garden. Hooray!!! Think good snail-y thoughts tonight, Diary.

Chapter 13

Holy Cannoli!

CANNOLI = Yummy Italian dessert with a creamy center

Tuesday

Guess who got asked for fashion advice . . .

Coco_Lulu_msg

Lulu: Hey Coco, what 2 wear 2 veggie grdn planting?

Kiki: what u wearing 2day?

Coco: gardening gear, of course...

This is Lulu's idea of gardening gear.

Sure the cargo pants have lots of pockets for gardening tools, BUT they are made out of <u>satin</u>! And the gloves are lined with fake fur—I can't wait to see her dig in the dirt with those!

Kiki's outfit was only a little better.

VINTAGE = a fancy way of saying "old"

Her mom found those overalls in a **vintage** clothing store!

I just wore my usual: a faded tee and an old pair of jeans.

On my way to school, I texted Mika (and copied my LLGC girls).

Coco_Lulu_msg

Coco: wanna help us plant the garden after school 2day?

Lulu: u should totes come!

Kiki: pretty please!

Mika: tht would b so awesome! thx 4 inviting me! Have to run to class...Can't wait to plant veggies after school! TTYL

TTYL = talk to you later

Okay, so I know I said that yesterday was the Best Day Ever, but today was really the Best Day EVER! We all got As on our history project!!

Then after school, Uncle Nick helped us plant the garden (and by "us," I mean, us LLGC girls AND Mika, who got along swimmingly with a certain person whose name begins with "L"!). Cousin Nick, Aunt Nicolina, Nonna Nicci, Nonno Nico, and Cousin Nicola came to help out, too.

Then, Principal Morton came by and said,

"The snails that make this garden their home will be the luckiest snails on the planet!"

I couldn't agree with him more! Here's a picture of our garden:

Our Garden ♡

And you know what? I feel like the luckiest girl on the planet! I really am. For having such great friends who are willing to help me with anything . . . even when that anything is <u>snails!</u>

Soon after I got home, my father walked through the door. I ran to give him a hug.

<u>Cah-RUNCH</u> was the sound my hug made. I burst into tears. I totally thought I had squashed the snails he brought home!!!!!

The good news was that the sound was only me crushing the cannoli my father bought on his way home from the airport. Thankfully, there's no way to ruin cannoli. (Yum!)

I asked Dad where the snails were that he rescued because I couldn't wait to add them to the new garden. Then came the bad news:

"Sweetheart, I didn't bring snails home. . . . These were a very rare snail found only in the Amazon, and there were only two left of their kind. One was on one side of the island. The other was on the opposite side of the island. We were able to bring them together, but they have to stay there." – Dad

"So you kind of married them?" – me

"You could think of it that way." – Dad

Dad gave me a photo of the two snails.
I drew a wedding for them. See?

I told my dad all about the garden we had
made, and he came up with a great idea!

"Why not take snails from our backyard
to your new school garden? Our snails can
start new snail families there." – Dad

I better start collecting snails. If my
Italian snail family is anything like my
Italian real-life family, there are probably
at least sixty of them!

Snails are all collected and ready to go.
While I was counting them
(30, thank you very much),
I got to the number 13
and realized something.

13

Diary, today is your 13-day birthday!
Everyone knows that the number 13 is
bad luck. But I'm not afraid. I'm cured of
worrying about bad luck! Now I just have
to cure Nonna of worrying about it. . . .
And then maybe she'll let me adopt the
black kitty!

Chapter 14

My Lucky Cat

Wednesday

The LLGs got up early today to put the snail family in the school garden. On the way over, we saw Mika standing by her window. We invited her to come with us.

Pop Quiz: Guess Who Said It?

"mika, I'm sorry I haven't been so friendly to you. That wasn't fair because I didn't even know you. I'd like to get to know you better, though . . . if that's ok?"

? ? ? ? ?

EXTRA CREDIT: Guess Who Said This?

MI AMORE= Italian for "my love"

"Coco, **mi amore**, you are absolutely right. Superstitions can be silly. Please keep the kitty. She needs a home, just like everyone else. All I ask is that you do me one favor. Whatever name you give her, make sure it's lucky."

And that's when I decided what name to give the kitty. If you guessed Lucky, you are <u>correct</u>!

Now, Diary, TODAY was really the <u>BEST DAY EVER</u>! And the luckiest.

READ THE NEXT LOTUS LANE BOOK!

LOTUS LANE

Lulu

BRANCHES

My
Glamorous
Life

Kyla may

SCHOLASTIC

Kyla May

lives near the beach in Australia with her husband, three daughters, two dogs, two cats, and four guinea pigs.

Like Coco, Kyla loves animals. Unlike Coco, Kyla is not a great cook. But thanks to Kyla's husband, family, and friends, delicious food is just a meal away. One day Kyla hopes to become an awesome cook . . . as soon as she finds a really cute apron to wear.

Kyla's first passion is drawing. Her second is chocolate.